The Extraordinarily Ordinary Life of Cassandra Jones

Walker Wildcats Year 1: Age 10

Episode 3: Road Trip

The Extraordinarily Ordinary Life of Cassandra Jones
Walker Wildcats Year 1: Age 10
Episode 3: Road Trip

Tamara Hart Heiner

Print edition
copyright 2015 Tamara Hart Heiner
cover art by Octagon Lab
Illustrations by Elisa Allan

Also by Tamara Hart Heiner:
Perilous (WiDo Publishing 2010)
Altercation (WiDo Publishing 2012)
Deliverer (Tamark Books 2014)

Inevitable (Tamark Books 2013)
Lay Me Down (Tamark Books 2016)

Tornado Warning (Dancing Lemur Press 2014)

TABLE OF CONTENTS

Episode 3: Road Trip

CHAPTER ONE

Family Vacation

"We have an announcement to make," Mr. Jones said as the family sat down to the traditional spaghetti Sunday dinner.

Cassie perked up. The announcement. Her dad had mentioned last night that he had a surprise, and she'd been anxiously waiting since then. She glanced at her mom. Was she finally pregnant? She'd been trying for so many years, everyone had kind of given up on the idea. "What is it?"

"Hold your horses," her mom said, extending her hands out to the children on either side of her. "After prayer."

Cassie obediently took her mother's hand in her own and her sister's hand with the other. Once everyone's hands were held, her father bowed his head and said a blessing on the food.

"Amen," Cassie echoed, then lifted her head to study her mother. "Well, what is it?" She ignored the bowl of spaghetti that came her way.

"We're taking a family vacation later this month."

"But we have school," Emily said. "How can we go on a vacation?"

"Well, we'll have to pull you out of school. That will be okay, right?"

"Yes!" Scott cheered. Just six years old, he hated everything school related.

"Vacation, that's cool," Cassie said, finally piling some noodles on her plate. Hopefully Ms. Dawson, her fifth grade teacher, wouldn't mind. She added some sauce and cheese to the noodles. Personally, she liked vacations in the summer time. She could go to the pool, hang out in the sun. With Thanksgiving just weeks away, she didn't consider this prime time to travel or play. But who was she to complain? "Where are we going?"

"Well, your aunt and uncle in Georgia invited us to have Thanksgiving with them. We thought, since we're going to be driving that far south, we would just make a trip of it and go to Florida, too. Maybe go to Disney World again."

Cassie stopped with a forkful of food almost in her mouth. Emily coughed on a swallow of water and sputtered, "Disney World? I've always wanted to go there!"

"Me too!" Scott said.

Even little Annette got involved, shouting, "Yeah, me too!"

"Well, everyone's been before except Annette," Mrs. Jones reminded them all. "You just don't remember because you were little."

"I remember," Cassie said. "I remember lots of it." But the memories were hazy, foggy, like looking in the mirror after a shower. She couldn't be sure what was real and what was her imagination.

"I don't remember anything," Emily said.

"Don't expect it to be anything exciting," Mr. Jones said. "In fact, maybe we should just skip the whole Disney part. Really boring."

His statement was met with loud cries of dismay, and he grinned. "Or not. Then be sure and tell your teachers. We leave in a week."

"Wait, what about Scaredy?" Cassie said, her eyes widening in alarm as she thought about her dog. "We're not leaving him behind, are we?"

"Relax, honey," her mom said, patting her hand. "We have a sitter for both dogs and the cat."

Of course. Cassie nodded. She should have known they'd thought of that.

♥

"Disney World!" Danelle squealed. She

5

handed her milk carton to Cassie, who always needed more milk at lunch. "That's so awesome! I've never been!"

"It's going to be cold," Riley said matter-of-factly. She primped her short, strawberry-blond hair with the palm of her hand and then picked up a sliver of bell pepper. "You won't have fun."

Cassie wrinkled her nose, both at the smell of the peppers and at Riley's words. Danelle and Riley were her best friends and had been since she moved to Arkansas earlier this year. But the two girls didn't really like each other. As far as Cassie could tell, there was no real reason behind it, except that the dislike began in preschool and continued to this day. So Cassie always felt stuck in the middle, figuratively and sometimes literally.

"Those stink," she said, referencing the peppers.

Riley leaned closer to Cassie and took a big bite. "Mmm, yum."

Cassie pulled her head back. "How do you know it's cold? Have you been to Florida in November?"

"No. I don't want to, either. Sounds boring."

"Boring?" Danelle said, arching an eyebrow. A little bit heavier, Danelle was a complete opposite to Riley's petite frame. "Who doesn't want to go to Disney World? Oh, wait, I get it. You're jealous." She whispered loudly to Cassie, "Riley always acts this way when someone else is getting something she can't have."

Riley's cheeks turned beet red. Her nostrils flared, and Cassie knew she wanted to throw

7

something at Danelle.

"Why don't you like Disney?" Cassie asked, trying to dig them out of the angry feelings swirling around them.

"It's for little kids," Riley snapped. "Are you a little kid?"

Danelle hooked an arm through Cassie's and tugged her toward her. "How would you know, Riley? It's not like you've ever even left Arkansas."

That intrigued Cassie. She and her family had moved here from Texas, so she had at least those two states under her belt. Not to mention all the other ones her family had visited. "Really? You've never been out of Arkansas?"

"Who cares?" Riley bit down hard on another pepper. "I've got everything I need right here."

Danelle huffed and mumbled something under her breath.

Riley stood up, holding her lunch tray close to her chest. "I'm done eating."

"I told you," Danelle said. "I told you she's annoying and immature. If she doesn't like something, she tries to make other people feel bad."

"How can you possibly know that?" Cassie shook her head. "You went to the same preschool. She's hardly the same person."

"Yeah? She seems the same to me." Danelle pulled a toothbrush out of her purse. She always brushed her teeth after lunch, or food got stuck in her braces. "I'm excited for you. Buy me something nice."

"Thanks, Danelle," Cassie said, glad at least one of her friends was happy for her. She didn't always understand Riley. They were in the same Girls' Club after school, and they got along great—most of the time. Sometimes it seemed Riley decided she couldn't stand Cassie anymore, or she was tired of her. And the mood swings often blind-sided her.

♥

Ms. Dawson approached Cassie on Friday with a stack of papers. "You said you'll be gone for a full week?"

Cassie looked at the papers and gulped. She gave an apprehensive nod. "Yeah. Well, a week of school, and then the week of Thanksgiving. We start driving today." Ms. Dawson hadn't said anything about homework, and the closer it got to the end of the day, the more hopeful Cassie had become that there wouldn't be any.

"Well, I wrote down all of your

assignments." She handed Cassie the top sheet, which had columns broken down into days, books, and page numbers. "That will get you through the week. And here are the worksheets you'll need to do." She placed the rest of the papers on Cassie's desk.

Cassie nodded, trying not to look too disappointed. There would be plenty of time on the drive down to Florida for her to work on this stuff.

"Have a blast!" Ms. Dawson said, giving her a smile. "We'll see you when you get back."

She said goodbye to her friends before she got on the bus, even though Riley had remained cool and distant all week.

"I'm serious!" Danelle said. "Bring me something cool!"

Cassie laughed and hoped Danelle wasn't

that serious, because she didn't have money to buy things.

Her dad was home when the bus dropped Cassie and her siblings off. All doors and the trunk of the van were open as he loaded it up for the trip. "I need your suitcases," he said. "Put whatever you're going to use to entertain yourselves in the seats next to you. Don't forget pillows and sleeping bags."

Cassie retrieved her suitcase, packed the night before. She opened her fun bag and made sure it had everything she needed for a two-day drive. She had five of her favorite books, stencils, and a collection of brain-teaser puzzles. Cassie opened her backpack and added her homework to the fun bag.

The blanket on her bed moved, and Scaredy poked his head out. Cassie petted his nose, letting him lick her hand. "Don't forget me while I'm gone," she murmured.

She carried her things out to the car, then went back to her room to give Scaredy a big goodbye hug. "Be good for the babysitter. I'll see you when we get back!"

CHAPTER TWO

Car Trouble

It was a full two hours later before everyone was finally in the van. Mr. Jones was yelling, Emily was crying, Scott was complaining, and Mrs. Jones just put on her seat belt, leaned her head back, and shut her eyes.

They backed out of the driveway, and Mr. Jones launched into a tirade about being ready on time and following instructions. "This will be a lousy vacation if I have to yell at you kids every five minutes for not doing what I told you!" He made eye contact with every child in the rear-view mirror.

Nobody said anything for the first twenty minutes of the drive. Cassie entertained herself with her puzzles, and even felt some contentment at the thought of the hours in the car ahead of them.

Not Scott. "Why aren't we flying?" he asked, just half an hour into the trip. "It would be so much easier."

"Way too expensive," Cassie said, knowing the answer before her father could say it. "Just going to Disney is expensive."

"And we're going to two different places," her dad said. "We'd have to fly to Florida and fly home from Georgia. Airlines don't like to do that."

Twenty minutes later Scott was grumbling again. "How much longer?"

"Well, we've been driving less than an hour," Mr. Jones said, an edge of irritation in his voice. "So we have about six hours left for today."

"That's too far!" Scott groaned.

Cassie wished desperately for some headphones. She could tell already this was going to be a long journey.

The first day of driving was uneventful and dull. Cassie started out strong doing her homework, but after about half an hour, she tired of it.

They crossed over into Tennessee and then

Mississippi. Cassie fanned herself, noting that it was warming up in the car. "Daddy," she said, "it's getting hot back here."

"Turn the AC on, Jim," Mrs. Jones said.

"You do it," he replied. "I'm driving."

A moment later the cooler air began to kick out of the vents above Cassie's seat. "Must be nice weather outside," she said.

"Must be," Emily agreed. "I see the sun shining."

They listened to an audio book and endured Scott's constant nagging before finally reaching a hotel around ten at night.

Nobody was excited the next morning as Mr. Jones marched them into the car around six a.m. "Just eleven more hours," her mom said as everyone got seated. As if that was supposed to be reassuring.

Cassie ate her morning pop tart and went back to sleep. When she woke up, two hours had passed. She immersed herself in her stencils, and then started reading her second book. When she finished it, she sighed and tossed it on the seat beside her. Nothing was fun right now, not even reading. "What's that smell?" she asked. At first she had thought it was someone's barbecue, but as it got stronger, it just smelled like something burning.

"Jim, pull over," her mom said, placing a hand on his arm and pointing out the window. Little puffs of smoke billowed up from the hood. Her dad grumbled something and Cassie sat up straighter, trying to see over her siblings' heads in the middle row.

"Is the car broken?" Emily asked.

"Let's hope not," Cassie said, consulting the

watch on her wrist. They'd only been driving for five hours. They were nowhere near their final destination.

Mr. Jones got out of the car and propped the hood up. Cassie undid her seatbelt, and her mom whipped around.

"Do not get out of your seat!" she ordered.

Cassie made a face and redid her seatbelt. A few minutes later, her dad got back in.

"I think it's overheating," he said. "I need to get it to a mechanic to look at."

Her mom looked around, and Cassie did too. They were on a highway somewhere in Georgia, with nothing around except thick trees, the colorful leaves still making their lazy descent from the upper branches to the ground. There weren't even any road signs or other cars driving around.

"Well, I guess we better pray it makes it to the next exit," Mrs. Jones sighed.

The next exit sign appeared ten minutes later, along with the words "No Services" written across the bottom. Mr. Jones put his blinker on, the steady *click click click* reaching all the way to the back of the car.

"Don't take that exit!" her mom snapped. "There's no services! We'll just waste our time driving around!"

He took of the blinker.

Five minutes later another sign appeared, this time with a few unrecognizable restaurants and gas stations listed.

"It's not really smoking anymore," Mr. Jones said. "Maybe it was just a piece of leaf or something that caught fire and had to burn off."

"If you think so," Mrs. Jones said.

"Yeah, I think we're good."

Cassie relaxed and pulled out another one of her books. She knew she should work on her homework, but that wasn't nearly as interesting as reading. "Crisis averted," she told Emily. "The car's fine."

"Are we there yet?" Scott asked from the middle row.

"I'm hungry!" Annette announced for the hundredth time.

"Cassie, snacks," her mom said.

Cassie leaned over and opened the big green cooler between the two rows. "Grapes, anyone?"

As she handed out the green globes, she thought she smelled smoke again. She sniffed the air. "What's that smell?"

"Jim!" her mom exclaimed.

The tires squealed as the van veered to the right. Cassie grabbed onto Annette's chair as the car came to a screeching halt.

Without a word, her dad got out and rounded the car. Mrs. Jones sighed, and Cassie finished handing out the grapes. She sat back and watched her dad pop the hood. Small ribbons of smoke rose up around him.

He closed it and got back in the car. "Let's just sit for a bit," he said. "It needs to cool off."

This was definitely not fun. It was one thing to sit in a car for hours knowing they were getting closer to where they wanted to be; it was quite another to sit for hours and go nowhere.

Plus it was getting toasty in here. Cassie pushed up the sleeves of her shirt and fanned her face. Her mom rolled down the windows.

After about twenty minutes, Mr. Jones turned the engine on again. They sat for a few minutes, waiting for him to make his verdict. Cassie sniffed the air. She didn't smell any smoke this time. The engine emitted a deep hum, but otherwise seemed fine.

"All right, I think we're good." Her dad eased their way back onto the interstate.

"We have to get to a mechanic before we go home," Mrs. Jones said.

"I know, I know. First thing tomorrow."

"How much longer?" Scott whined.

"Six more hours," Mrs. Jones said.

Six more hours. That would get them there around eight o'clock tonight. When they left the hotel, they'd hoped to get there a little before seven. Already lost an hour.

Cassie turned back to her book. She wiped her brow and realized she was sweating. "It's hot back here again."

"It's really hot, Jim," her mom said.

"Well, you want me to focus on driving, or making the car comfortable?"

She exhaled loudly and leaned over the controls. "It says the AC is on."

"Then it is."

Cassie put her hand up to the vent. "It's blowing air. It's just not cold."

Mrs. Jones punched a bunch of buttons. "It's not working."

"Has to be. It was working fine earlier."

"That was before the car started smoking, wasn't it?"

The two of them bickered back and forth. Cassie tried to tune them out and concentrate on her book. She didn't want to think about how hot it felt back here.

Mr. Jones pulled the van over, and Cassie looked up. "Why are we stopping?"

"The van's smoking again," Mrs. Jones muttered, pressing her fingers to the middle of her forehead. Cassie hoped she wasn't getting a headache.

They sat and waited the prescribed twenty minutes, and then her dad started the car up again.

It continued that way for the next several hours. They'd drive a half hour, one hour at the most, and stop when the car started smoking. The heat became unbearable, and her mom gave them permission to get out of the car when they stopped.

When they finally pulled into the campsite,

it was after ten p.m. Cassie was hungry, hot, and grumpy.

"Let's get the tent up," Mr. Jones said, hauling out the large fabric bag.

"It's late," Cassie said, swatting at a mosquito. "Can't we just sleep in the RV?"

"No," he said. "This was the arrangement you wanted. You girls in the tent, us in the RV."

It had sounded like a fun idea last week, inside their chilly house in Arkansas. Now it sounded miserable. "We can put it up tomorrow. Right, Emily?"

"No, let's sleep in the tent," Emily said.

Cassie groaned. "Mom, I'm tired. I just want to lay down."

Her mom paused, the big green cooler in her arms. "Jim, just let them sleep in the RV tonight."

27

"But I don't want to!" Emily exclaimed.

"They don't want to," her dad echoed.

"I do!" Cassie said. But it didn't matter. Her dad and Emily had already started setting up the tent. Cassie blinked back tears of frustration and went to the car. She waited until the tent was up, then pulled out her sleeping bag and pillow.

"Good night, girls," her dad said. Everyone else was already in the RV, probably sleeping now, feeling the artificial cool air generated by the air conditioner. "See you in the morning."

Cassie crawled into the tent, fluffed her pillow, and didn't bother answering. What a miserable start to their vacation.

CHAPTER THREE

Magic Time

"Well, I don't know what to tell you folks." The mechanic stuffed a greasy rag in the pocket of his overalls, then removed his baseball cap and scratched his balding head. "I don't see anything wrong with your car."

"Be quiet," Cassie told Scott and Annette for the hundredth time. She was trying to listen to her parents and the mechanic, but it was hard to hear over her brother and sister's giggling. They jumped around the old tires where her mom had left Cassie in charge. She grabbed Annette's arm as she ran by and yanked her down. "You're supposed to be sitting still!"

"There has to be something wrong," her dad was arguing. "All the way from Georgia, we were stopping to let it cool off because it was overheating. It doesn't take a mechanic to know that a car in good condition doesn't do that."

The man shrugged. "I'm sorry. I mean, you can leave it here if you want. But other than maybe an oil change, I don't know what else we could do to it."

"Let's just go," her mom said, hands on her

hips, a visor shielding her eyes from the bright Florida sun.

"Here." Mr. Jones paid the mechanic and gestured to the kids. Annette and Scott took off for the car.

"Come on, Emily," Cassie said, nudging her sister's foot. "We're finally going to Disney World."

"Yay," Emily said, putting her book away.

They pulled out onto the highway, following the big signs that beckoned them to the land of Mickey Mouse.

"So what happens if the car breaks down on the way home?" Cassie asked.

"We do what we did on the way here," her dad said shortly. "And take it to a real mechanic when we get home."

All of Cassie's concerns about the car faded

away, however, as they approached the Disney gates. Familiar characters and princesses decorated the booths, and though Cassie didn't squeal or bounce in her seat like Annette, her pulse quickened in excitement.

"We're here!" Emily cheered.

"Yeah!" Scott yelled, and everyone joined him, even her mother.

They parked the car and got out, and Cassie couldn't take her eyes from the beautiful sculptured shrubs, or the long line of people waiting to get in.

"I want to see everything," she said, feeling her face split wide with a grin. "We can't miss anything."

"Don't worry, we'll see it all," her mom said.

"Where's the castle?" Emily asked. They

followed the crowd of people, handing over their tickets. "I don't see anything."

"That's because we're not at the park," Mrs. Jones said. "We're at the station. From here we can take the monorail or the ferry to the Magic Kingdom."

"The mono-what?" Cassie asked. She didn't remember as much from the first visit as she'd thought. Everything looked unfamiliar and new. Then again, she'd only been four years old.

"The monorail," her mom said. "It's a train that connects the parks. We hop on the station here and can take the train to Magic Kingdom or to EPCOT, or even some of the hotels on Disney property."

"A train?" Scott's eyes looked ready to bug out of his head. "I wanna ride the train!"

33

"The train, the train, let's do the train!" Annette squealed.

"Yeah, that sounds fun," Cassie said, and Emily nodded.

"This way, then," Mr. Jones said, gesturing for them to follow him up the ramp. They stood in impatient anticipation as the monorail finally appeared in the distance, a train shaped more like a speeding bullet. It came to an abrupt stop in front of them, and all along the sides, doors slid open.

"This is awesome!" Emily giggled, climbing on.

After a moment, the doors closed, and the train sped off again. Scott stared when the tracks led them right through a building.

They arrived too soon for Annette and Scott. "Can we go again?" Annette begged.

"Please?"

"We will when the park closes," Mrs. Jones said.

"Guys, it's not even a ride," Cassie said, anxious to leave the station behind. "The real stuff's still in front of us. Look!" She pointed to Cinderella's castle, just looming in the distance. The blue towers stood out against the slate walls, and Cassie found herself wishing more than anything that she could climb those towers. She remembered fantasizing about being a princess when she was a little girl. Now here she was, all grown-up and still wanting to see the world from the top of a castle.

"Wait till you see Main Street," Mrs. Jones said. She and Mr. Jones exchanged a smile, and she took his hand.

They walked through the gates and came

out in—a town? Cassie blinked in surprise at the quaint buildings nestled up against one another, a cobble street paving the way between them.

"Shops," her mother explained. "But isn't it beautiful?"

"Amazing!" Cassie said. Her gaze remained transfixed above her, staring at the decorate lettering over the doors. Candy shop, Barber shop, toy shop, holiday shop, bakery, ice-cream shop. Her stomach rumbled appreciatively. "Let's get started!"

♥

The lines weren't too bad this time of year, but the Joneses still had to deal with some wait time. Cassie's favorite was the dwarf mine ride, a little roller coaster that played through the scenes of "Snow White." Annette liked "The

Little Mermaid" ride the most.

For lunch they ate at Geppetto's Workshop, a cafe made to look like it came out of the "Pinocchio" movie. Maybe Cassie was just starving, but she thought the soup in a bread bowl was phenomenal. She ate every last bit, savoring the bowl after the soup was gone.

"Magic Kingdom closes at seven," Mr. Jones said, spreading his map out across the table. "And there's a lot to see. I suggest we make an orderly trek through this part of the park, and when we run out of time, we hop on the monorail and head to EPCOT."

"Yeah, the monorail!" Annette said.

"What time does EPCOT close?" Cassie asked, sitting up straight and looking at the map with her father.

"Nine o'clock. And they have a really fun

fireworks show that you kids will probably like."

"We better get going," Mrs. Jones said. "Time's ticking."

The next few hours flew by. Her dad gathered them up before the crowds started and herded them to EPCOT, where Cassie had the best chocolate mousse with raspberry sauce she'd ever had in her life.

"Norway, huh?" she said, taking her last bite of mousse. "I'll have to go visit someday."

By the time she crawled into her tent that night, she couldn't care less where she was sleeping. Her whole mind buzzed with a happy energy, but her body collapsed in exhaustion. *What a perfect day*, she thought.

CHAPTER FOUR

Rainy Days

Cassie dreamed she was swimming. She knew it was dream because never would she go swimming in all her clothes, and in her dream she was sopping wet in a shirt and jeans. She dove into the pool and came out shivering. She picked up a towel to dry off, but it was wet too.

"I can't get warm!" she said to no one. Her teeth chattered with the cold.

"Cassie."

Cassie opened her eyes to see the dark shadow of Emily above her, shaking her shoulders. "Cassie, wake up."

"What's wrong, Emily?" she murmured. Abruptly she realized how cold she was. And wet. No wonder she'd been dreaming about swimming.

"It's raining and the tent's soaking. What should we do?"

Cassie sat up, hearing now the tinkling of the rain as it fell on the canvas. Moisture gathered in small drops on the inside of the fabric, dropping on them when gravity became too difficult to resist. Water seeped into the tent from the ground, and the sleeping bags were drenched.

"Argh!" Cassie exclaimed. She picked up her bag of clothes, hoping something inside would be dry. "Let's get in the RV!"

Emily grabbed her stuff too and both girls tumbled out of the tent. Cassie protected her head with her bag and rapped on the RV door. "Mom!" she shouted.

"Daddy!" Emily added.

No response, and Cassie banged harder. The rain continued to pour around them, and she trembled. "Mother!" she hollered.

The door opened, and Mr. Jones stood in the doorway, the RV dark behind him.

"Come in, come in," he murmured, his voice thick with sleep.

"Gotta get out of these clothes," Cassie said. Her father vanished into the bathroom and came back with towels.

"What's going on?" Mrs. Jones asked, coming out of the back bedroom.

"It's raining and the girls are wet." He looked around the RV. The couch was already made into a bed, and Scott and Annette slept there. "I think the table folds out."

Cassie found a dry shirt and pants to put

on. By the time she finished getting dressed, her dad had the table made into a bed. It was small for the two girls, but it was dry. "Change, Emily," Cassie said to her sister, who still stood there in her sopping clothes. Half asleep, Emily started changing.

Mrs. Jones went back to the bedroom, but Mr. Jones waited until they had crawled into the bed. "Are you warm?" he asked.

Cassie fluffed the towel under her head and nodded, tiredness pulling at her eyes and making her head feel heavy. "Yeah."

"Mm-hmm," Emily agreed.

"Good. We'll see you in the morning, then."

❤

The rain had lessened by morning, the steady downpour replaced by a gloomy drizzle. The temperature had dropped as well, and Mrs. Jones made everyone wear sweaters under their rain jackets.

"It was so warm yesterday," Cassie said, wrapping the sweater around her. "How did it get cold?"

"It's November here, too," her mom said, zipping Annette's jacket. "It might not get as cold, but the weather certainly cools off."

The entry gates with the colorful Disney characters greeted them, cheerful even in the cloudy mist.

"Can we take the monorail again?" Scott asked.

"No," Cassie said, still determined to try everything at least once. "Today we need to take the ferry!"

"Fairies are for girls!" Scott said.

"I love fairies!" Annette said.

"Not that kind of fairy," Emily said. "A ferry like a boat."

"It's a boat?" Scott asked, still looking uncertain.

"Yep," Cassie said.

"I guess that's fine, then," Scott muttered, looking down at the toy transformer in his hands like he didn't want to admit he was pleased.

It was cold. Cassie shivered as they got out of the van. She wanted the warm sunshine from yesterday. They got on the ferry and moved to the front. A little girl about Cassie's age sat on a bench, her hands clutched around her father's arm. Cassie gave her a smile and the girl smiled back. She leaned toward her dad and said something that Cassie didn't understand at all.

Cassie sat next to her father and tried to eavesdrop on their conversation, but no matter how she strained her ears, the words didn't make sense to her. "Are they speaking another language?" she asked her dad.

"They're speaking Spanish," he said. Then Mr. Jones turned to the man and said something. The two conversed in Spanish for a bit.

"Cassie," Mr. Jones said, taking her hand and pulling her in front of him, "say, '*Como te llamas?*'"

Cassie looked at him, not sure she could repeat those sounds.

"*Como te llamas*," he repeated. "Say it to the little girl."

Cassie forced a smiled and pronounced, "*Como te llamas*?"

"*Maria*," the girl said. Her black eyes glittered when she smiled. "*Como te llamas*?"

Cassie turned to her father, not sure what to say now.

"She just told you her name," he said. "And then she asked yours. Answer her."

"Cassie," she said.

The girl said something else, the separation of the vowels and consonants completely lost on Cassie.

"What did she say now?" she asked.

"Ask her," her father prodded.

Cassie sat back down, flustered and embarrassed. "I don't understand Spanish."

"She said, 'nice to meet you.'" Mr. Jones said something to the father, and the two men laughed.

Cassie didn't try to speak again, but she

listened to the exchange between them. They said goodbye when they got off the ferry.

"She seemed nice," Cassie said.

"You should have tried to talk to her more. She was excited to talk to someone."

"I don't speak Spanish."

"I could teach you."

Cassie considered that. "It's a very pretty language. It all blends together, kind of sing-songy. Sounded like they were singing."

"Yes, you're right. Spanish does sound like a song."

Cassie paid more attention after that. She noticed several times when she thought she heard people speaking Spanish, and other times when she couldn't tell what language it was. Maybe someday she'd have to learn another language.

♥

No one took any chances on the rain that night. Mrs. Jones spent the last hours of the evening at the laundromat, drying the sleeping bags for Emily and Cassandra. Then the girls joined the rest of the family in the RV, warm and cozy on their table-turned-bed.

"What was your favorite part about today?" Cassie whispered. She could hear Annette and Scott breathing deeply at their end of the RV. They had fallen asleep almost as soon as they laid down.

"The Japanese restaurant," Emily whispered back. "I love watching them cut up and cook our food. And it's the first time I've eaten with chopsticks."

"Yeah, that was awesome," Cassie agreed. So far, the food had been one of the highlights of the vacation. As long as she had good food to eat, she was happy.

"What about yours?" Emily asked.

"I don't know. Maybe meeting Maria." Even though she hadn't been able to talk to the girl, she hadn't been able to get her off her mind. "I wish I had a way to talk to her some more. I should have gotten her address. We could be penpals."

"Maybe you'll see her tomorrow," Emily murmured. Her words slurred together as her mouth grew too tired to open.

"Yeah, maybe," Cassie said, but she doubted it. Tomorrow they were going to the water park, and she had a feeling it would be cold. She suspected her family would be the only one crazy enough to be there.

But even if she didn't see Maria, she liked

the idea of a penpal. She decided to meet someone else from another country and exchange addresses. What fun it would be to get mail from somewhere outside of America.

CHAPTER FIVE

Abandon Tent

The water park didn't open as early as the other parks, so the Jones family ate breakfast inside the trailer.

"The sun's out," Mrs. Jones said, putting the milk back in the refrigerator.

"That doesn't mean it's warm," Mr. Jones said, sounding grumpy. "It's about sixty-five degrees outside."

"Is that cold?" Cassie asked.

"It's warmer than yesterday," her mom said. "Do you not want to go, Jim?"

"I never said that." Mr. Jones put on a baseball cap and walked out of the trailer.

"Is he mad?" Cassie asked.

"Just tired. Vacations wear on him."

Cassie couldn't understand that. She was tired, but vacations were fun, weren't they?

♥

Cassie loved swimming. She could spend all day at the pool, doing nothing but underwater handstands and splashing around.

By the time they got to the water park, however, it had started to rain again. She stood under the cabana her mom had claimed, teeth chattering as she shivered out of her shirt and placed it on the table.

"But it's raining," Scott was saying as he clutched his towel to his chest.

"And you're going to get in the water. You'll be wet anyway. Stop complaining." Mr. Jones pulled Scott's shirt over his head. "If no one wants to be here, we'll just pack up and head back right now."

"No, no, we want to be here," Cassie said. She rubbed her bare shoulders, trying to erase the goosebumps popping out all along her arms. "The lazy river looks fun. Come on, guys." She forced herself to walk away from her towel, though she was so cold her body ached.

"Cassie, keep Annette with you." Mrs. Jones gave Annette a little shove, and Annette's skinny legs ran her over to Cassie. She had on her floaties.

"Stick close by," Cassie told her. "I don't want to lose you."

"We're like the only ones here," Emily murmured, grabbing an empty intertube and handing it to Cassie.

"But not quite. See? There's people." She pointed to two teenage boys a ways ahead of them on the river. Cassie put Annette in the tube and climbed up beside her. Both of them lifted their legs up, keeping as few body parts in the water as possible.

Scott and Emily got in their own tube and pushed off behind Cassie.

She couldn't get warm. She shivered and rubbed her arms. Her teeth chattered, and she cringed anytime the water touched her. She looked at Annette, her lips trembling and blue.

This isn't fun, Cassie thought.

A tunnel appeared up ahead, with a waterfall flowing across the opening. Cassie groaned. The only way onward was through the water. She tried to push the intertube to one side so they wouldn't get as wet, but the resulting cascade didn't seem any less than it would have been. The dark tunnel was even colder than the open air, and Annette began to cry.

"It's okay," Cassie told her. She touched her sister's freezing skin. "We'll be out soon."

Nobody said a word as they reached an exit to the lazy river. All four of them ascended the steps. Cassie imagined her expression matched the grim faces she saw on her brother and sisters.

"I just want to dry off and go home," Emily

said.

"We should at least try the slides," Cassie said, not quite ready to give up on the day. "Don't they look fun?"

Annette's teeth clattered together, the remnants of tears in the corners of her eyes. "N-n-no."

"I'll go with you," Scott said.

"I can't leave Annette."

"I'll take her back to Mom," Emily said. "We'll sit and wait."

"Okay." Cassie started for the tall slides, wishing the sun would come out. Even for just a little bit. It would make all the difference in the day.

They climbed to the top of the platform, following the small line of other people who hadn't realized how cold it would be today. A wind blew across them, and Cassie couldn't stop shaking. She felt like she'd never be warm again.

Scott went first, and Cassie watched him disappear with the first dip in the slide. She sat down in the shallow pool at the top. The frigid water tickled her thighs, promising more icy delights to come. She could chicken out, get up and go back down the steps.

"Your turn," the boy running the slide line said.

Just get it over with. Cassie sucked in a breath and pushed off. Instantly the air pressure knocked her against the slide. She crossed her arms over her chest, helpless as the water splashed her face, her arms, her neck, places that she had managed to keep dry up until now. Then the slide ended, and she plunged into a pool of water. She shot her feet down and found the bottom, then pushed her head out with a gasp and a sputter.

Scott waited for her at the side. He took her arm and helped her out. Cassie shook from head to toe.

"All right," she said between clenched teeth. "I think I'm done."

♥

The only thing everyone wanted to do after the water park was take a nice, hot shower. Mrs. Jones refused to let everyone use the tiny shower, so Mr. Jones led them down the trail to the shower house closest to the RV.

Cassie stayed in the shower longer than necessary. The hot water steamed up in the stall and billowed around her. She closed her eyes and waved it in her face, inhaling the misty warmth. Slowly the cold infused in her bones started to peel away.

"Cassie?" Emily called. "Annette went back with Daddy. I'm supposed to wait for you. Are you almost done?"

She did not want to be done. But the shampoo was out of her hair, and her body no longer felt cold. She turned the water off and counted to five before opening the stall door. The chilly air blasted over her, and she jerked the towel around her body, rubbing her skin and drying off as quickly as possible.

"Should we sleep in the tent tonight?" Emily asked.

Cassie pulled on her pajamas. "No way. I only just got warm again."

"Yeah. Me too."

They trooped back to the RV, where Mrs.

Jones was setting the table for dinner.

"Mom," Cassie said, "I don't think it's a good idea if we sleep outside. It might rain, and everything will get wet again."

"That's fine," her mom said. "Just sit down and eat."

♥

Cassie woke up in the morning to see her dad emptying the cupboards and packing things up. She rubbed her eyes and sat up. "That went by fast."

"Yep," he said. "Vacations usually do. Next stop, your cousins' house."

Cassie waited her turn to use the bathroom, then packed up her clothes. Her backpack fell on the floor, and she paused to examine it. The heavy text books inside reminded her of all the homework she hadn't yet done. "I'll do it on the drive to Georgia," she promised. She headed outside to help load up the van.

The day looked like it would be warmer than the previous two. Already the air held the promise of heat, the little teasing kiss that made her want to shed her sweater. The sun crowned on the horizon.

"Looks like we went to the water park on the wrong day," she said to Emily, joining her at the van.

"I hated yesterday," Emily said. "I wish we'd gone back to Disney World."

"Yeah. But we didn't have any more tickets." It hadn't been enough. She hoped they'd come again and stay longer next time.

CHAPTER SIX

Thanksgiving

Cassie held her breath the whole way to Georgia that the car would make it. Surprisingly, it didn't start smoking once. Maybe the mechanic had been right and there really wasn't anything wrong with it.

It was late evening by the time they arrived. They parked in the long driveway, and before

Cassie even had the chance to get out of the car, her cousins spilled out the side door. She'd seen them a few years ago at a family reunion, but she couldn't remember their names. She climbed over the cooler and got out.

"Hi," she said to the girl. "I'm Cassie."

"I know who you are," she replied. "You're my cousin."

Yes, but Cassie was drawing a blank as to her name. "And you're. . . ?"

"Carla," she said with a scoff. "You don't remember our names?"

All three of them stared at her now, and Cassie glanced around for her mom. But her parents had gone into the house, their arms laden with luggage. "Sure, I remember. You've just changed, and I wasn't sure who was who."

"Oh, okay." That seemed to satisfy her.

"Bring in your stuff, and I'll show you where you're sleeping."

Cassie got her sleeping bag and duffel bag. After a moment's hesitation, she grabbed her backpack. She'd only spent about half an hour on her homework today. She'd probably have the chance to do more here.

"Everyone can come," Carla said, directing her siblings to help get bags. "You're all sleeping in the same place."

"Okay," Cassie said. She nodded at Emily. "Emily, Annette, Scott, come on." She followed Carla into the garage and up a set of stairs, then through the kitchen and into a big room on the other side.

"This is where y'all will be sleeping," Carla said.

Cassie dumped her sleeping bag against the

wall. Two big televisions faced the room. "What do you usually do in here?"

"It's the game room. The boys play video games on that screen and we watch movies on that one." She pointed out the different screens. "The boys will probably be in tomorrow morning to play. This is where they hang out."

"Oh. Great." Cassie nodded. "Thanks."

"Yeah. We'll see you in the morning." Carla backed out of the room.

One of the boys who looked a little younger than Scott was showing off a toy.

"That's awesome!" Scott said. "Does it transform?"

Cassie hid a smile. Scott wanted everything to transform.

"No. It's not a transformer. I have a great video game, though. I'll show you tomorrow."

"I love video games!"

Not Cassie. Big waste of time, if anyone asked her. She hadn't gotten a great "welcome" vibe from Carla. Cassie had a sudden longing for her own bed, her own room, her own dog. She unrolled her sleeping bag and curled up inside.

♥

Boring.

That was the best word to describe hanging out at Carla's house.

The younger boy invaded the guest room before Cassie was even awake, turning on the video game. The gaming started before breakfast and showed no signs of stopping.

Cassie got dressed and ate cereal. At least they had a good selection. Her aunt and uncle were there, but no sign of Carla or her brother.

"Where's Carla?" Cassie asked, putting her dirty bowl in the sink.

"Around here, we take care of our dirty dishes," her uncle Gary said, stopping her before she left the sink. "You need to put your bowl in the dishwasher."

"Oh." Cassie blushed under the chastisement and retrieved her dirty bowl. She carefully lined it up in the dishwasher. She was almost afraid to ask again, but she did anyway. "Where's Carla?"

Her uncle walked out of the kitchen, and her aunt said, "Probably in her room."

"Thanks," Cassie said, and she hurried away, wondering why her mom's relatives were so weird.

She had never been upstairs before but figured Carla's room must be up there, since nothing else was down here. She ran into her parents in the front room, sitting and reading.

"Hi," she said, joining them.

"Hi, dear," her mom said, putting a book down. "Why aren't you with Carla?"

"I think she's still sleeping," Cassie said. "I haven't seen her yet today."

"Well, go play. Once we start making food for Thanksgiving, you won't have the chance to hang out."

Go play. Such great advice. If only she could find something to do. "Okay." She climbed the stairs and paused at the top. A bathroom and three closed doors faced her. She knocked on one door and pushed it open.

"This is my office," her uncle said, not even turning around in his leather chair. He sat with his back to her, typing away at a computer.

"There's a game room downstairs and a living room and a library. Find somewhere else to play."

Cassie closed the door quietly, not bothering responding. She felt like a nuisance in this house. She gave up looking for Carla's room and went back to the guest room. With nothing else to do, she pulled out her backpack and selected a homework assignment.

How utterly shameful, when she was resigned to do homework for entertainment.

♥

Nobody gathered for a formal lunch. Cassie wandered into the kitchen when she got hungry, and her mom made her a sandwich. Then she put her to work peeling potatoes.

"Did you find Carla?" she asked.

"No," Cassie replied. She didn't elucidate

on the situation, either. She peeled potatoes, then peeled sweet potatoes, then helped roll out pie crusts. Slowly, her spirits began to rise. Tomorrow was Thanksgiving. She couldn't complain.

Her aunt prepared a quick meal of soup and crackers for dinner, and Mrs. Jones rounded up her kids. Cassie still hadn't seen Carla all day.

"Are your kids coming to dinner?" she asked Aunt Jadene.

Her aunt handed her a stack of bowls. "Put these on the table, please," she said. Then she walked over to a speaker in the wall and pressed a button. "Kids, we're eating dinner. Time to come down."

Cassie stared in fascination at the wall. "Is that an intercom?"

"Yes." Her aunt took the bowls from her and began to place them on the table. "It's quieter and more efficient than yelling." She gave Mrs. Jones a significant look.

"It works just fine in our house," Mrs. Jones said with a shrug. "Right, Cassie?"

Cassie much preferred everything about their house, all the way down to the endless amounts of noise. "I like it."

Aunt Jadene laughed. "Boy, you've got them trained, Karen."

At least we don't spend all day in our rooms, Cassie thought, but she said nothing. Especially when Carla and her brother trooped into the kitchen a moment later, disgruntled expressions on their faces. Scott and Annette came out of the game room with the youngest.

They said a blessing over the soup and

started eating.

"What have you done all day?" Cassie asked Carla.

"Just listened to music and written in my journal. It's been a nice, relaxing day."

"You should play with your cousins while they're here," Aunt Jadene said. "They won't be here forever, you know."

Carla looked at her mother and rolled her eyes. Her expression was easy to interpret: the sooner they're gone, the better.

Cassie couldn't have said it better herself.

♥

She spent Thanksgiving Day in the game room, learning how to play video games with her boy cousins. She was horrible at it. Even the youngest at three years old was way better than Cassie. And they had no patience with her.

Instead of giving her instructions on what to do better, they just yelled at her and told her to give them the controller.

Cassie only too willingly obliged them. She worked on her homework until her mom yelled, "Time to eat!" The intercom in the room buzzed with Aunt Jadene's voice: "Dinner is ready, everyone."

Cassie dumped her homework and scurried out of the room. Another table had been set up to accommodate all the food, and her mouth watered as she took it all in. There were her favorites, the must-haves at Thanksgiving: turkey, gravy, mashed potatoes, rolls. And a few items her aunt had added that she wasn't too sure about. And then, of course, the deserts: pumpkin pie, apple pie, cranberry pie, cherry pie. Cassie sat on her hands to keep from clapping.

"Before we eat," Mr. Jones said, coming up behind his wife and placing his hands on her shoulders, "we have a tradition in my family, if we may."

"Please," Uncle Gary said, motioning him forward.

"We always hand out to corn kernels." Her dad produced a small jar full of unpopped popcorn. "Everyone take two." He started with Uncle Gary. Carla looked at them suspiciously, but took two, just like everyone else.

Cassie knew what was coming. She took her two and beamed at her father. Now it felt more like home.

"Now I'm going to pass the jar around again, and you're going to put the kernels back. But as you do, say one thing you are grateful for with each kernel."

Cassie didn't pay much attention to everyone else's gratitude lists. She formulated her two in her mind, wanting to say something impactful, true, and profound. The jar appeared in front of her, and she dropped one in.

"I'm grateful to live in a country where we can safely travel whenever we want." She dropped in the other. "And I'm grateful for a family that understands me and supports me." *And I understand them.* She looked at her mother and smiled, ever so glad to be a Jones.

Available now!
Walker Wildcats Year 1
Episode 4: Fever Pitch

"How long have you been itching this spot on your head, Cassie?"

"Hm?" Cassie looked at Ms. Dawson and stopped scratching her forehead. She stood in line with her class, waiting to leave the cafeteria after lunch. "Oh. I don't know. I wasn't really paying attention."

"Ms. Wade, come here, please." Ms. Dawson beckoned to one of the other fifth grade teachers.

"What is it?" Ms. Wade asked, coming over.

"Look at this." Ms. Dawson pushed back Cassie's hair. "That spot on her forehead. She keeps scratching it."

"Well." Ms. Wade frowned. Cassie felt like a goldfish, the way the two women stared at her head. "What do you think it is?"

"How are you feeling, Cassie?" Ms. Dawson asked.

"Horrible," Cassie admitted. "I'm really tired and have a headache."

"Do you think it's the chicken pox?" Ms. Wade murmured, looking sideways at Ms. Dawson.

"I don't know. It's been so long since I've seen it." They both frowned at Cassie.

Cassie digested their words without comment. She'd heard of the chicken pox. Her mom had it when she was a girl, but Cassie had been vaccinated as a kid. She was pretty sure that meant she would never get the disease.

Ms. Dawson pressed the back of her hand against Cassie's forehead. "She doesn't feel feverish."

"Well, I guess we'll find out soon." Ms. Wade gave Cassie one last glance and returned to her class.

"Let me know if you start to feel sick, all right?"

Cassie nodded. She already felt sick, and she was pretty sure she'd said that, but maybe she needed to feel sicker.

She spent the rest of the day trying to keep her head up. Her eyelids drooped every time she started reading, and her head nodded while she tried to write out her answers. She couldn't focus on anything Ms. Dawson said, and she spent recess sitting on the sidewalk, bundled in her winter coat and her arms wrapped around herself.

Finally the bell rang signaling the end of school. Cassie moved as fast as she could from the classroom to the bus circle just so she could get on the bus first. She picked a seat by the window and leaned her head against it. Her vision blurred, and Cassie closed her eyes.

⚶

"Are you okay, Cassie?" her mom asked as Cassie dragged her feet in the door after school.

"No," she replied, too tired to mince words. "I'm going to bed." She dropped her backpack by the piano and went down the hall, not waiting for an answer. The pillow called her name. Her stomach tumbled over on itself, churning and grumbling. She wrapped her arms around her torso and curled up.

Cassie woke up, a bit groggy, her throat aching. She wasn't sure how long she'd slept. Her eyes slitted open. The weak light filtering through the blinds gave away that the day was ending, with night fast encroaching. Cassie sat up, her head heavy like it was full of cotton.

This end of the house was silent. She slipped out of bed and followed the murmur of voices to the kitchen. She wasn't hungry, though, so she sat down on the living room couch and watched her family eat.

Her mom noticed her first. "Hi, Cassie. Are you feeling any better?"

Cassie shrugged. "I think so." As long as she was sitting down, anyway, she didn't feel too bad. She lay down on the couch and rested her head on the armrest. She had an itch on her foot but was too tired to bend down and scratch it. She wiggled her toes, twisting her foot around to relieve the sensation.

If anything, the need only increased. Like a bunch of little ants walking in circles on the sole of her foot. And now they were tickling her with their little jaws.

Cassie grabbed her toes and tilted her foot so she could see the bottom. No little ants. She did notice, however, a tiny drop of water. She touched it with her finger and pulled her foot away. It wasn't water, but a small blister, and the moment she'd touched it, the itching had doubled. Now more than anything she just wanted to dig her fingers into that little blister and scratch it off. The first vestiges of panic crept up her chest. What was that? Leftovers from an ant attack? The beginnings of leprosy?

"Mom!" she called. "There's something weird on my foot!"

Her mom looked over from the table and frowned. "What is it?"

"I don't know." Cassie swallowed, trying to keep her voice calm. "Come see."

Her mom put her fork down, and the whole family stared as she made her way to Cassie. "It's all right, sweetie. What's on your foot?"

Cassie twisted her foot around so the bottom of it faced her mom. Then she held her breath as her mom's fingers traced the outlines of the tiny blister. It tickled and itched painfully, all at the same time. Then her mom's finger trailed down her foot and paused near the heel. The same sensation occurred, thought slightly less sensitive now.

"What are you doing?" Cassie pushed herself up so she could watch.

"You didn't notice this one, did you?"

"There are two?" Her heart skipped a beat.

"It's the chicken pox, Cassie. I'm pretty sure you've got the chicken pox."

The adventure continues with Cassandra Jones in sixth grade! *Walker Wildcats Year 2* available now!

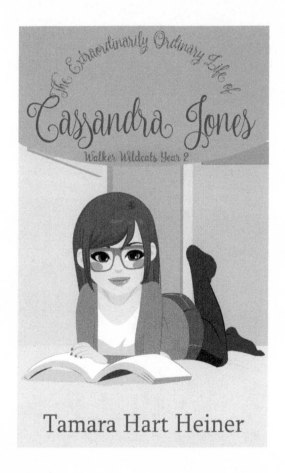

About the Author

Tamara Hart Heiner is a mom, wife, baker, editor, and author. She currently lives in Arkansas with her husband, four children, a cat, a guinea pig, and several fish. She would love to add a macaw and a sugar glider to the family. She's the author of several young adult suspense series as well as a nonfiction book about the Joplin Tornado, *Tornado Warning*.

Connect with Tamara online!

Facebook:

https://www.facebook.com/author.tamara.heiner

website: *http://www.tamarahartheiner.com*

Thank you for reading!

Made in the USA
Monee, IL
11 June 2022